The Meditation

These Words: Book III

A.E. Page

The Meditation (These Words: Book III)

Contents

Epilogue

The Meditation

Foreword

The meditation of our state and soul finds itself in two places: a place on the inside, and a place on the outside—inside, is a world of rumination, outside, is a world of reflection—two worlds on each side of a mirror, looking forth and back, exchanging their letters each minute of the hour. *The Meditation (These Words: Book III)* presents forty poems in two parts: *Part I. Letters of the Messenger*, exploring the endearment and evocation of letters, including: the addressing of others through love; and the addressing of experiences through life, and *Part II. Minutes of the Hour*, exploring the practices and peace of meditation, including: the slumbering of the mind; and the awakening of matter.

To Mum, Dad, Lauren, and family and friends, this book is dedicated to you.

A.E. Page

Part I.
Letters of the Messenger

A letter arrived at my door today; just what could it possibly say?

Prologue

For Those Dreamers With Their Heads in the Clouds

For those dreamers with their heads in the clouds,
where lines pave their silver upon skylines,
a vagrant voice wanders by through the crowds,
speaking words of wonder throughout its time.
Such words speak aloud, like an intimate
friend: all-knowing, all-seeing, guiding minds
to an end, an end which begins with fate
unbeknown, that sits in dreams undefined.
By the design of their own creation,
a dreamer can dream, as makers would make:
a world of their own imagination,
with most impossible things to awake.
And arise they shall, from slumbering thoughts,
that think, and ponder, on clouds that they caught.

Dearest love, these words I write are all for you, from a heart finding its way.

I.

Letters to Love

Even on a Darkest Night, I Know a Place Where Lights Still Shine

Even on a darkest night, I know a place where lights still
    shine,

through the curtains of a window drawn against a fateful sky,

as though they were a welcome sign, to come visit any time,

or a beacon on the horizon, guiding two feet on by.

Even on a rainy day, I know a place where souls still sing,

through the blusters of a tempest thrown against a sodden
    land,

as if to part the clouds themselves into the embrace of spring,

and walk amongst flowered fields, as a child with their
    parent's hand.

Even on a quiet morn, I know a place where words still
    speak,

through the soundscapes of a silence draped across a sleepy
    dawn,

as surely as the rising sun, wishing to garner a peek

into the lives of all those below, before the day is drawn.

Through the love of a mother, if there is something I have
    known,

even on an endless path, I know no place that is like home.

He Too Was a Boy Once, With His Hopes and Dreams

He too was a boy once, with his hopes and dreams,
packed into a suitcase far bigger than he.
So off they went together, into the stream
running down the causeway, out towards the sea.
Adventure was calling, and to it, he went,
one foot in front of the other, left, then right,
to the furthest reaches of the land's extent,
for out there, somewhere, lay an unblemished sight.
He may not have known it then, or even when
the land's end came, that feet would follow a heart.
But as tides have shown a time and time again,
all of a good thing returns back to the start.
After all of the things that have been and gone,
he too was a boy once, like father, like son.

It Is Magic–Pure Sorcery

It is magic–pure sorcery,
performed before these very eyes,
in all its shrouded mystery,
kept in secrets of sure surprise.
It is tricky–most difficult,
learning the art of something new,
like a child afront the occult,
and the spell that they almost knew.
It is priceless–ordinary
even–wondrous and glistening,
bound by the extraordinary,
as conjured up by a sibling.
They grab their books and read the words,
then venture off into their worlds.

I Remember All of You, When All of You Was Me

I remember all of you, when all of you was me.
That you are, and that I was: one of the very same.
I loved you then, as I love you still, stout-heartedly,
knowing I will be you, looking back at where we came.
Find me not among the white clouds of summer's ocean,
for some days are blue, and some days are grey in her mood.
Rather, look out and see me swim against the motion,
of her great waves, like razorblades, towards fortitude.
As I am shown where winds have blown, in glass reflections,
I am reminded of a time ago, where one stood
and looked up to a twilight sky of recollections,
then dared to dream of what had been, and its adulthood.
That I was you, and you were me, makes me think of days
lived in, and loved in, in so many different ways.

History Left Them Behind for Us to Carry Forwards

History left them behind for us to carry forwards,
as the custodians of a memory's museum.
It is with such a heavy load, we slowly head towards
the sunrise of tomorrow, and its fierce rays of freedom.
Somewhere along the trodden path the price to pay is steep,
trying to hold the weight of the world, as a sword of steel.
Though mountains climbed are far behind, the river runs
  down deep,
denying perdition its silence, on an iron heel.
That is no place for yesterday to linger all alone,
where ghosts are but an echo of a life lived long ago.
Within another minute, we might finally see home,
out there beyond the summit, besides somebody we know.
From highest highs, and lowest lows, the top to the bottom,
nobody gets left behind, and no one is forgotten.

Return Home When Pain Is Too Much

Return home when pain is too much,
and the feeling of yesterday
is but a wistful notion's touch
and notorious runaway.
Remember the old days fondly,
and once in a while, talk about
the time that ended most simply,
without any shadow of doubt.
If I were standing there again,
no longer would I wish to yearn
for either sunshine or the rain,
patiently waiting for my turn.
Then I come back from former times,
to knowing what I have, is mine.

Are You Who I Think You Are? Do You Remember Me?

Are you who I think you are? Do you remember me?

We used to go to school together; funny, I say:

of all the people, of all the places, here, I see

the past return, as if it were only yesterday.

Those birds that sat up on the roof, well, they flew elsewhere.

That cat that used to prowl the streets, now it sleeps indoors.

Those children who used to chase cars, now they watch and
stare.

That friend you sat next to in class, well, they wanted more.

Yet here we are, as though time still wants to play with us,

and a playground's game goes unfinished from way back
when:

when we were young, and we were stronger, without a fuss,

when days were longer, with time enough to play again.

Now, close your eyes and count to ten, then, where will we
view?

Do you remember me, just as I remember you?

Dearest Love, Who Knows Me Better Than I

Dearest love, who knows me better than I,
my tongue is tied, when tender confessions
stand alone to declare, or at least try,
to say their words in laboured possession.
It is you, who even in bleak winter's
beauty, can melt away the coldest heart,
raging on through as an ardent splinter,
embedded deep down into the rampart.
And as if to distract a burning ache,
there comes a feeling much like ecstasy,
to numb a pain stretching out in its wake,
as a poison would seep its penalty.
If love could not love because it was real,
then life would not hurt, yet, nor would it heal.

Should These Words Be Read by Someone I Have Never Met

Should these words be read by someone I have never met,

then I shall know a happiness that few have since found,

and should these words find meaning somewhere I have not
crept,

then I shall walk much further than these two feet are
bound.

Maybe in these places we might meet face to face, and

I can speak of something I have being meaning to say,

and maybe between the spaces I might lend a hand

to anyone, and everyone, who has been this way.

It is simple really, to enjoy a life's pleasure,

looking up to the clouds on a bright and rainy sky,

but it is simple also, to look down and treasure:

a letter, a word, as it brings a smile, low and high.

Dear, reader, whoever you are, wherever you are,

these words are for you, however close, however far.

Dearest life, these letters I send are all for you, sealing in moments of time.

II.
Letters to Life

Silence Sings at the Start With Ease

Silence sings at the start with ease,
but in its song finds its own voice,
to talk to the trees, birds and bees,
as Mother Nature would rejoice.
Into the night, into the day,
a traveller roams, brave and bold,
in search of words of which would say
the greatest story never told.
The world beneath the feet swings by,
faster, faster, with us on top,
and yet for all that we might try,
one day it will come to a stop.
Slowly, surely, nothing is left,
aside a song of birth from death.

In Other Words, You and I Are Rather Quite Alike

In other words, you and I are rather quite alike:
two people on a planet far much bigger than us.
I speak my voice, and you speak yours, on an evening's hike,
neither one understanding of what we might discuss.
We walk upon the same green grass, see the same blue sky,
we breathe in the same crisp air, and feel the same brisk
  wind,
but there remains a difference between you and I,
and it is to this difference that we are both twinned.
For these words, we each have one, and together that makes
two: two of us to read and write, in so many ways.
And how many more there must be, to give and to take
a myriad of meanings in what we have to say.
To our conversation, we arrived from where we came.
In other words, you and I are rather quite the same.

Leave the Present Behind, and Take the Old With the New

Leave the present behind, and take the old with the new,

that there might then be a past to learn and a future

to find: yesterday, and tomorrow, in the same view

of a window looking out upon a world's décor.

A castle once stood over there, tall and proud and strong,

now all is earth and stone laid bare across the field tops,

and so there rests its story, and so there rests its song,

to sing throughout the centuries, sowing in the crops.

Harvest time is near, the sheafs are turning into gold,

so is the time to collect a treasure to adorn:

our histories, our heralds, our halls in which we hold

the legacies of heritage, from which we are born.

The old ways show a path, it is a choice to follow,

entering a new way another might then borrow.

A Letter From the Messenger

A letter from the messenger
arrived this morning at my door.
It fell silent as a feather,
as it landed upon the floor.
I know well its writing, on its
paper coat, keeping warm the cold:
a most fashionable outfit,
that can be given, but not sold.
Confessions of raw feeling, fine
and fearless, forgo afterthought.
Captured is a moment, of time
itself, in every line and blot.
Such is a thing received from you.
As for now, I shall write one too.

The Possibilities Are Endless

The possibilities are endless
in a life that seems, to me, so short,
as I enter a room to undress
and try on the clothes that I have bought.
Some fit nicely, some are far too tight,
others are far too loosely fitted,
some are far too dark, or far too bright,
but nonetheless, I stay committed.
That reflection inside the mirror
looks back to see what is going on,
watching plays of trial and error
learn to walk before they then can run.
What would I be, if not but myself?
Sitting, far up, on the highest shelf.

Company of Friends

Company of friends,
most true, ever kind,
each meet at the end,
for us to remind.
Solitude has found
me, inside the wild
of my wood. Unbound,
we both sat and smiled.
This day will go soon,
somewhere far away.
Before we cocoon,
let us go and play.
Now, a memory
makes two: you, and me.

A Way Wind Has Whispered Across the Land

A way wind has whispered across the land,
sweeping its coat in a greatest assault.
The world keeps on turning, and here, I stand,
astride a colossus that cannot halt.
This thief has found something worth the plunder:
a simple thing that cannot be returned.
The skies creep closer in all their thunder.
Oh, little me, how the tables have turned.
Once, I thought I knew everything there was.
Now, knowledge is a power to behold.
The sunshine sets on every one of us,
leaving behind a day to then uphold.
Goodbye sadness, for we have loved too long.
Goodbye sadness, ever old, ever young.

Where Was I When I Came to Lie?

Where was I when I came to lie
upon the soft shore serenely?
I remember clouds floating by,
passing the days most dreamily.
Might I have walked across the sands
of a very familiar place?
Only, tide and time have brushed hands
over footprints without a trace.
What a curious thing indeed,
to have found happiness, but then
to have lost it, which, I concede,
could so surely happen again.
So I shall walk back into bliss,
wherever true happiness is.

If Tomorrow Does Come, What a World It Will Be

If tomorrow does come, what a world it will be:
an uncharted country nobody has travelled,
dressed in surprise, and embellished in mystery,
that not even time itself has yet unravelled.
This world grows small now, as its candlelight sinks down,
into a basin of a melted, waxen floor.
Contempt to fall asleep, it dons its nightly gown,
bidding its leave unto the stranger at its door.
Will it be golden? Will it be grand? In this world
that I head onto. Will I come to understand
the question to ask, upon the illusion curled,
before tomorrow's conclusion is close at hand?
What shall happen shall happen, amongst everything,
if tomorrow does come, what a world it would bring.

Now I have sent this letter of mine, I eagerly await your reply.

Epilogue

Where Do We Go From Here, When We Have Reached the End?

Where do we go from here, when we have reached the end,
and the longest journey seems like a second's thought?
Does the answer lie ahead, to find and ascend?
Or is the question waiting to be asked and sought?
Let me find my own way, to find out for myself,
for if I do not, how will I learn what can be?
Could it be something? Could it be nothing? Itself,
or something else? What would these two eyes of mine see?
In endlessness, possibilities rise, higher
and higher than the stars that shone. Shining once more,
an ending must come, and decision made prior
to the departure away to the furthest shore.
Where do we go from here, when we know not what comes,
but towards an ending, which at one point, begun.

Part II.
Minutes of the Hour

One minute, one hour, one moment to spend.

Prologue

Slumber

Life
lies down
for a rest,
retreating—with
me.

Curtains close to the rest of the world—and the rest is all behind.

I.

Minutes to Slumber

Breathe

In
and out
to the song:
a metronome
heart.

Ground

Firm
beneath
the bottom,
and two feet on
it.

Space

Veil
covers
pull the light,
to an endless
space.

Float

Light
as air,
floating off
without care—or
thought.

Balance

Slow,

steady,

one by one,

stacking stones on

top.

Repose

Soul
beheld
the body:
not a word did
speak.

Source

The
river's
rain raptures
—water leaves the
jug.

Respect

Gift
of what
was given,
and earned, without
cost.

Relax

And
relax:
each minute
of the hour goes
by.

Life returns back to the body, and finds itself anew.

II.

Minutes to Awaken

Movement

First,

fingers,

and then toes,

bringing life—on

back.

Body

Free
to be
whoever,
with all that makes
us.

Mind

Thoughts
pass by,
showing eyes:
all inside the
mind.

Focus

Who
never
wanted one
thing, more than a
wish?

Conscience

I
look forth
and back—the
mirror has: two
sides.

Compromise

Dreams
conjured
the moon, but
arose to the
sun.

Release

Leaves
of the
autumn shade:
letting all things
go.

Teach

Sown
is the
seed, so that
the blossom may
bloom.

Moment

The
dawn sun
rises—for
a moment, so
close.

Find yourself here, and find yourself there, in and out across two worlds.

Epilogue

Awaken

Eyes
open,
wide and wake:
I find myself
here.

Appendix

Poems

Forms

- Lantern: one stanza of five lines, metre of 1-2-3-4-1, and no rhyme. Line 5 relates to Line 1, and topics are based on a single idea. Themes vary. From Japan.
- Shakespearean sonnet: one stanza of fourteen lines, any metre, and A-B-A-B/C-D-C-D/E-F-E-F/G-G rhyme. Stanzas comprise of three quatrains and a couplet, metres remain consistent, and often, even-numbered syllables are stressed, and odd-numbered syllables are unstressed. Themes vary. From England.

Printed in Great Britain
by Amazon

37953502R00047